All Aboard!

100 years of Trams, Trolleys and Buses in Cardiff

CARDIFF
CAERDYDD

Cardiff Bus
BWS CAERDYDD

South Wales
ECHO

TransBus
International

Message from the Lord Mayor of Cardiff

PUBLIC transport has long been one of the defining issues of local government. In 1902 municipal leaders of the then Cardiff County Borough acquired Cardiff Tramways to meet the transportation needs of a rapidly expanding urban area. One hundred years on, Cardiff is seeking to develop a transportation infrastructure fit for the 21st Century.

If the lesson of history is that transport makes or breaks cities, then local people can take confidence from the fact that Cardiff has a proud record in this area. The establishment of the Cardiff Bus Company was a bold and imaginative step. It reflected clear understanding of the importance of public rather than private solutions to the problem of moving large numbers of people from the suburbs to the urban centre. Routes needed to be planned in a coordinated manner to address the genuine needs of communities.

Cardiff Bus has always provided a vital service for the City - and it represents one of the few remaining municipal bus companies in the UK. The result is that Cardiff is better placed than most cities to provide a modern, but equitable, public transport infrastructure. There are major challenges ahead, with a projected increase in private car use of 30% over the next ten years. The role of Cardiff Bus will be more important than ever, particularly as the Council leads moves to develop a top-class transportation system for Cardiff and Wales.

Councillor Russell Goodway
The Rt Hon Lord Mayor of Cardiff

Foreword: *Dan O'Neil*

CARDIFF'S great docks, its factories, its foundries and railways, its theatres and shops and suburbs, its triumphs and its wartime traumas, the histories of all these have been chronicled over the years.

But one part of our city's past has been sadly neglected. Until now. Time then, to welcome a long overdue and loving, look at what unromantic souls would doubtless call our Public Transport System.

Which is like trying to sum up the Mona Lisa as a mixture of oil, paint and canvas. For when, on May Day, 1902, the Mayor and Corporation clambered, like eager schoolboys, aboard a dozen glittering new electric tramcars outside the Town Hall, they were as wide-eyed with wonder as the rest of the town.

So how the crowds turned out to gape at those "swaying, gliding galleons of the streets," a famous description which only hints at the magic.

A new century. A new era. And all through it the city's growth could be reflected in the changing ways its people went to work.

Hard to imagine, now, what the town was like when one thousand horses hauled five hundred open topped "buses" through our streets. But easier when you see these old photographs.

Look, too, at the photographs of those first gaudy tramcars, and you can almost hear them clattering, see the sparks fizzing from the new fangled electric wires and the clashing, iron wheels.

And who can doubt the smug feeling of progress being made when the first motor buses arrived in 1920, or when Cardiff welcomed the double-deck tramcars three years later, a boon on wet days for the upstairs only smokers.

In these pages you will see the city saying farewell to its trams in 1950 after welcoming its trolley buses in 1942. You will be told how they worked and who worked them and, most important of all, who used them, more than 18m passengers in the first year alone.

And then, perhaps you will see how crucial they have always been for millions in the century since that memorable May Day.

Contents...

P7 Chapter 1
In The Beginning

P11 Chapter 2
The Great War and the Roaring Twenties

P18 Chapter 3
The Thirties and the Depression

P24 Chapter 4
World War II and the Forties

P31 Chapter 5
The Fifties - A new era

P38 Chapter 6
The Buses in the Swinging Sixties

P44 Chapter 7
Pick up a Seventies Orange

P50 Chapter 8
The Twentieth Century Draws to a Close

P56 Chapter 9
Into the Twenty-first Century

Introduction

Solomon Andrews embraced medicine, undertaking, furniture, shops, department stores, cinemas, skating rinks, colleries, car hire and garages. And tram and bus services

The opening of Cardiff Tramways horse tram service from High Street to Pier Head in 1872. This view in High Street shows the fashions of the time and the arrangement of seats on the top of the tram. The horse, obviously keen for the off, is not as transfixed by the camera as its human companions.

Amongst many other things, Solomon Andrews built buses and trams, and this is one of his Patent Omnibuses of 1882. These were very advanced having improved access to upstairs and the back wheel clearing the bodywork without the need for a wheelarch.

THIS book is a celebration. It celebrates one hundred years of transport in Cardiff, as seen through the eyes of local people and told through the history of the City's own bus company - known recently as Cardiff Bus.

By offering a snap-shot of life in Cardiff, the company's history and demonstrating how transport affects the lives of everyday people, this book chronicles the enormous impact that the arrival of horseless-buses had on the development of Europe's youngest capital city.

The River Taff leaves the South Wales mountains through the Taff Gorge. 2000 years ago a hamlet grew on the swamps where the river met the sea. In the second half of the 18th Century, coal and ironstone were discovered in the hills starting a huge export business. Transport was needed and the only route was via the gorge reaching the sea at Cardiff. Mules were used first, the Glamorganshire Canal came in 1794 and the Taff Vale Railway in 1840. Bute West Dock opened in 1839 and Cardiff's population of 8,000 in 1836 was 123,000 by 1888. A town built on transport soon needed its own.

Horse buses first appeared in 1845 followed by horse trams in 1872. There were many providers, a major one being Solomon Andrews. From Wiltshire, he settling in Cardiff in the 1850's, and founded interests as far afield as Australia. Starting as a baker and confectioner, he embraced medicine, undertaking, furniture, shops, department stores, cinemas, skating rinks, colleries, car hire and garages. And tram and bus services. In addition to Cardiff, he had tramways in Pwllheli, Leicester and Gosport. On 25 July 1898, Cardiff County Borough (as it had been since 1889) was taking an interest and obtained Parliamentary powers to take over tramways in the Town. On 1 January 1902, Cardiff Tramways, part of Provincial Tramways, was acquired, £65,644 being paid for the lines, 52 cars and 342 horses. The story of Cardiff's passenger transport had begun.

Chapter One: *In The Beginning*

By 1905, 131 electric trams were at work

When the new electric trams were delivered, they arrived at Roath railway sidings along the road from the depot. Temporary track was laid on the road and the trams were partly dismantled for transporting, having their top decks replaced in the depot.

CARDIFF set about converting the trams to electric power. The first General Manager, Arthur Ellis, was appointed in 1900 to do this and made his first report on the options for power supply equipment and its siting on 14 September, one week after arriving in Cardiff. On 2 May 1902, the last horse tram routes were replaced by electrics, although it wasn't until October the 17th that the last horse drawn tram ran.

On 18 September, a purpose built depot to hold 94 trams was opened at Roath next door to the electricity generating station. It's position was chosen to be near the railway for delivery of coal and near Roath Brook for the supply of cooling water. At noon on 10 February 1903, the Cardiff Docks and Penarth Harbour Tramway was bought for £12,000, adding the Adamsdown to Grangetown route and work commenced to convert it to electric operation this being ready on 9 February 1904. By 1905, 131 electric trams were at work. Horse buses were still in evidence, the last one running to Penarth on 2 October 1909.

Motorbuses appeared in 1907 but were not allowed to run in the City by the Council. Proposals to run buses as far as Merthyr were mooted and the Council relented and allowed such vehicles in from 1910 whilst remaining solely a tram operator itself. In 1913, Cardiff, the largest coal exporting port in the world, handled 13 million tons of coal.

The official reception for the opening of the electric tramways took place on Thursday 1 May 1902. It was held outside the Town Hall in St Mary Street using 12 tramcars that were seen as a huge technological advance. The first one was driven to Canton by the Mayor.

The trams' progress through St Mary Street was unimpeded by other traffic, unlike today. Like today, the sight of a camera turns people's heads. Tram 11 passes the Town Hall in 1902 shortly before the building was replaced by the magnificent new civic centre in Cathays Park.

The docks were the focal point of public transport in Cardiff for many years. This 1902 view of the Pier Head landing stage looks towards Bute Street and tram 30 is waiting to depart for the town centre. Solomon Andrews & Sons' offices are on the left and, 45 years later, Cardiff's distinctive single deck trolleybuses would reverse to the right. P & A Campbell's paddle steamers departed from this pontoon carrying many who had arrived by tram to such places such as Weston super Mare and Ilfracombe. The company allowed employees of the Tramways Welfare Club a 33 1/3% discount on its boat fares.

In 1905, Cardiff became a City and was entitled to a Lord Mayor. Tram 34 passes the junction of Cowbridge Road and Llandaff Road in that year. It is working the Canton to Pier Head route which ran every 4 minutes until 7.30 pm, then every 5 minutes to the Monument, every 10 to Pier Head thereafter. The central overhead wire supports are very distinctive and ornate.

I remember when...

WHEN she got on a tram to pop into town in 1947, Dorothy Adams did not imagine that it would be the start of a 54-year journey.

But the Cardiff local admits she has had the ride of her life since meeting her husband on the trams all those years ago.

Husband Ernest used to be a conductor on the trams in Cardiff and got talking to Dorothy one day when she got on his tram with bandages on her legs.

"I'd been to Barry Island for the day and had been bitten by sand-flies," said Dorothy.

"I told Ernest and that broke the ice. He then asked me out on a date."

Even then, Ernest knew he and Dorothy would be together for a long time.

"When she got off the tram, I went through to Bert Evans, the tram driver, pointed her out and said 'that's the kind of girl I want to marry," he said.

"And I did, two years after that meeting."

Chapter Two: The Great War and the Roaring Twenties

MANY staff were lost in action during the Great War and workshops were used to produce munitions. Post war, servicemen returned having been taught to drive by the Army and there were lots of ex army vehicles surplus. Many bus companies were set up and there was much competition, often not to the Corporation's benefit. In this environment, on 24 December 1920, Cardiff started to run its own motorbuses. Driver only single deck buses started running to Llandaff North and Llanishen on 7 May 1923 and later to Radyr and Morganstown. Expansion outside the City grew with a service to Newport starting on 15 April 1924 and one to Caerphilly on 13 May 1929. Trials with pneumatic tyres were successful and on 15 February 1929 authority was given for Dunlop to equip 15 vehicles at £94, 18 shillings and 7 pence each and one by Goodyear for 1 penny less. Mr R. L. Horsfield left as General Manager at the end of September 1928 and 28 applications were received for his replacement. This was reduced to a shortlist of 4 who were interviewed each receiving £5 expenses and first class train travel. William Forbes from Aberdeen was appointed at a salary of £1,150 p.a. On 2 February 1929 agreement was reached with the Great Western Railway to meet their excursion trains and travel to all parts of the City for 6 pence, however agreement was refused for fitting cigarette vending machines to buses and trams.

By 1928, Cardiff had one of the largest fleet of municipally owned motor buses in Britain and things looked bad for trams. The planned extension to Ely was questioned in July 1927 with the cost of

Women were employed on the trams for the first time in World War I. A total of 200 were working by 1918 when tram 36 is seen. As resources were diverted to the war effort, maintenance reduced, track deteriorated and only 80 of the 131 trams were usable. The ladies did not get a smooth ride.

reaching Wilson Road put at £59,000. By 17 May 1929, the General Manager was recommending not to proceed. A more serious situation had occurred on tram route 1 from Whitchurch Road to the City and Docks. This needed single decks to pass under the Salisbury Road bridge and the Great Western Railway had refused to raise it and to lower the road would risk flooding. The General Manager recommended replacement of 12 trams with 10 new buses "to provide a better service."

Trials with pneumatic tyres were successful and in 1929 authority was given for Dunlop to equip 15 vehicles at £94 18s 7d each and one by Goodyear for 1d less

Competition and the need to buy out competitors after WW1 caused the Corporation to start running motorbuses on 24 December 1920. The first six were Dennis Stevens petrol electrics, a very unusual type, with 28 seat bodies by Dodson. They were numbered 48 to 53 and used on the St John's Square to Monthermer Road route and number 52 is seen here in Penywain Road. They lasted between five and nine years.

Cardiff was plagued by low bridges, one leading to the first tram route withdrawal. The Corporation's General Manager, Mr R.L.Horsfield, designed a special type of low height, covered top tram to combat this and the first one, 101, here new in February 1923, is crossing the magnificent Clarence Road Bridge over the River Taff. It cost £1,735, in contrast five old trams were sold on 20 November 1929 for £162 and 10 shillings. 101 was built to a high standard, weighed 10 tons and was 14' 10" high, 29' 6" long and 7' wide. The electrics came from BTH, the chassis from Peckham and the body from Brush of Loughborough. It was very successful and a further 80 were ordered. The last new trams for Cardiff, single deckers, came in 1927, bringing the fleet to a peak of 141. Mr Horsfield went on to Leeds where he produced yet more successful trams.

On 1 October 1922, the Corporation took over operation of the Cardiff Tramways Company's services to Whitchurch that had not been included in the 1902 deal. The Corporation's first double deckers were introduced on this route. Number 62, one of the first, is seen and was of the rare Dennis Stevens type, only Walsall Corporation buying similar. The Dodson body seated 52. They lasted for eight years compared with the expected life of 25 years for a tram.

MARTELL BRANDY

150

The Corporation's first covered-top double decker motorbus started work on the Whitchurch route on 24 October 1925. Number 150 (UH 81), the second, a Dennis with 50 seat Dodson body is here in Kingsway in 1930, after being fitted with pneumatic tyres. It wasn't until January 1931 that bells were fitted to the upper deck.

With William Forbes shown as General Manager, Dennis 224 of 1929 is seen in Loughborough at the Brush bodyworks when brand new in 1929. 10 of these had been ordered at £830 for the Dennis chassis and £770 for the Brush 46 seat bodies. When it was agreed to replace the route number 1 trams, Mr Forbes asked how much reduction he could get for 20 buses instead of 10. Brush reduced the price by £7 10 shillings per bus but Dennis would not budge. 30 extra bus drivers were required at a training cost of £155. 224 lasted until 1938.

The General Strike of 1926 caused much disruption. No Corporation buses or trams ran on 4 May but on the next day a limited service was run by volunteers. There were incidents, pickets disconnected the petrol supply from one bus and tried to remove the driver from another. Police intervened and buses proceeded. Number 81 a Northern Counties bodied Dennis 52 seater, is seen here manned by volunteers and draped with the Union Jack.

I remember when...

John Hall could have been the first casualty of the Second World War if it weren't for the quick reactions of a Cardiff tram driver.

For in his rush to cycle home after hearing that war had broken out on Sunday 3 September 1939, John fell off his bicycle straight into the path of an oncoming tram.

"The front wheel of my bike caught in the tram line and I went head over tip," said John, from Heath, Cardiff.

"As I looked up there was a tram bearing down on me at a fair speed. It was terrifying but thankfully the driver managed to bring it to a screeching halt about a foot away from my legs."

After his lucky escape, the driver took John to hospital where the nurses patched him up.

As he stumbled home to Trafalgar Road, Roath, he was greeted by crowds huddled in the street.

"I thought they'd heard about my accident. But no... all the talk was about the war and how everyone thought it would be over by Christmas."

John served four years in the Royal Navy between 1942 and 1946, but says his close encounter with the tram remains one of his most shocking moments of the war.

Chapter Three: *The Thirties and the Depression*

With the expanding motor bus fleet, a new depot was proposed to hold 106 of them in Sloper Road. The council's direct labour department built the foundations and Archibald Dawnay & Sons of Cardiff had their quote of £23,900 and 10 shillings accepted for the building

**INSET PICTURE:
Fare list 1929**

ROUTE 1 trams were replaced by buses on 5 January 1930.
The annual renewal of licences that year for the tramway covered 199 drivers, 405 conductors and 134 trams at a cost of £61 2 shillings. To curb competition, the 1930 Road Traffic Act was enacted to licence routes and on 20 March 1931, the General Manager was authorised to make the necessary applications to the new Traffic Commissioners. The Great Depression reduced income considerably and the Council cut wages. Producing fuel from coal was examined, and authority was given on 12 October 1931 to borrow a bus with a diesel engine. In 1932 diesel engines were fitted to two buses and all subsequent deliveries had them, the whole fleet being fitted by 1944. The docks remained important and transfer fares for workmen were introduced to allow a change of bus, for example Splott to Pier Head for 3 pence in January 1930. With the expanding motor bus fleet, a new depot was proposed to hold 106 vehicles in Sloper Road. The council's direct labour department built the foundations and Archibald Dawnay & Sons of Cardiff had their quote of £23,900 and 10 shillings accepted for the building. £420, 10 shillings and 11 pence was paid to

allotment tenants as compensation and a valuation of garden produce on the site and work commenced on 19 May 1930. The Lord Mayor, Mr RG Hill Snook officiated at the opening at 12.30pm on 29 July 1931, later treating guests to tea at the Wenallt. All did not go entirely to plan, later in the day a bus caught fire and caused £252, 10 shillings worth of damage to the roof of the new depot.

In January 1936 a report was given to the Transport Committee on the effects of traffic congestion in the City centre and in February one on the effects of a Severn Bridge scheme. Later that year, one of the very advanced AEC 'Q' type buses was bought. It had a side mounted engine, front door and pre-select gearbox, and demonstrated how forward looking Cardiff was. There was a major conversion of tram routes to motorbuses on the Roath Dock and Clive Street to Splott routes on 11 October 1936 despite the fact that the single deck trams used on them, some of Cardiff's finest, were only nine years old. Some were later sold to a company in Brazil. In 1939, after much debate, the remaining tram routes were planned for conversion to trolleybuses, continuing to use locally produced electricity.

Church Parade. June 20th 1926

The Cardiff Corporation Transport band seen on the Law Courts steps on 20 June 1926. In the 1930's they won numerous prizes including at the national band finals in Crystal Palace. On 7 July 1931, the band approached the Council over replacement of instruments at a cost of £544, 19 shillings and 9 pence, with a discount of £143, 16 shillings and 9 pence for cash. 500 staff had agreed to contribute one penny a week from wages to repay the debt. The council agreed to advance the money and to contribute one pound for every pound contributed by staff.

Thornycroft number 44 (UH 8234), new in 1930 has a 52 seat body by Hall Lewis. This official Thornycroft photo shows it in Kingsway on the Cyncoed route when new. It soon became 254, then 28 and lasted until 1943.

One of the most famous and revolutionary buses of the time was the Leyland Titan with Leyland 48 seat body. In 1929, Cardiff borrowed this one, UH 7175 and in 1931 purchased it. Here it is seen with some splendid period advertising in the background in St John's Square.

A typical Cardiff bus of the 1930's this AEC Regent with Northern Counties bodywork of 1935 was one over 60 similar. There was huge debate about whether to replace trams with trolleybuses or diesel buses and it seems likely that the transport department favoured a standard fleet of these flexible buses. In the end trolleys were chosen but the fact that they largely did not extend beyond the old tram routes probably contributed to their demise. Number 18 is in Westgate Street.

A calm if rainy day in 1938 at Victoria Park tram terminus. The bus on the right in this picture is on a connecting service to Ely. Trams never made it there, but from 1955, trolleybuses did. In the next year, the decision would be taken to scrap the trams and also Britain would be plunged again into War. This delayed plans and gave the trams an 11 year extension of life. Trams and buses had their own sequence of numbers. This is tram 18, above it is motorbus 18, both running at the same time. Just as well they ran from different depots.

From an early date, Cardiff buses ventured out into the surrounding countryside. This 1937 AEC Regal 149 with 35 seat Northern Counties body is at Clawdd Coch near Pendoylan on the 32 service. The bus received perimeter seating during the war increasing its capacity to 58. The rural nature of the route is clear. It was an extention of the route from Westgate Street to St Fagans which bus 18 is seen working on page 22. In 1954 it was extended to Hensol Castle without needing extra buses but was abandoned in 1971 when the Council felt it could no longer use City ratepayers' money to subsidise a loss making route outside the City.

I remember when...

Cardiff Bus put women in the driving seat during World War I, giving society a glimpse of the true potential of women as equals.

For the first time it was normal and quite acceptable to see women working as drivers and conductors on trams around Cardiff.

And in driving women to the forefront of a male-dominated world, the bus company played a pivotal part in one Cardiff family's history.

For it was while Gladys Forrest was driving her tram that she met her future husband, Guy.

"My mother was driving a tram through Cardiff when she had a slight accident with a taxi, said her son, Norman.

"The driver of that taxi was my father!"

Gladys and Guy married shortly afterwards in 1917 and were happily married for over 50 years.

But the circumstances of their first meeting were always a source of light-hearted dispute.

"My parents used to laugh at their funny meeting, but neither of them would take responsibility for the accident that brought them together," added Norman.

"My dad always said it was my mother's fault, but she argued that it couldn't have been as her tram was on rails."

Chapter Four: World War II and the Forties

On 25 August 1939 it was agreed that in a National Emergency, fuel consumption would be halved and powers sought to run trolleybuses everywhere. On St David's Day 1942, the first trolleys replaced trams on the Wood Street to Clarence Road route

AIR raid precautions and the operation of a gas decontamination machine were under way late in 1938 and by December of that year, 71 employees were in the Homeguard. The Council voted in favour of converting the remaining tram routes to trolleybuses on 8 May 1939 but their introduction was severely delayed by the war. On 25 August 1939 it was agreed that in a National Emergency, fuel consumption would be halved and powers sought to run trolleybuses everywhere. On St David's Day 1942, the first trolleys replaced trams on the Wood Street to Clarence Road route every five to six minutes, being extended to Llandaff Fields on 8 November every 10 minutes at peaks, 12 off peak. They introduced a pay as you enter flat fare system. The buses were built to pre-war standards although the amount of wood was restricted and the cost of equipment increased by 10% due to the War. The War resulted in the curtailment of services. Those to Llandough, The Drope, Thornhill, Newport, Peterston, Penarth, Markham and Merthyr being affected from 8 September 1939. There were increased accidents during the blackout, in one month increasing by 10 over the equivalent period. After seven weeks of blackout it was agreed that conductors be reimbursed for any wrong coins collected in the darkness. Speedometers were illuminated from March 1940 and the pay and conditions for employing women noted. Bus windows received netting and blackout material, and crews requested the issue of helmets, gas masks and torches. To save fuel, experiments were made with gas power but only four buses were fitted. On 2 January 1941, the administrative office in Paradise Place was destroyed by bombing and most records lost. Temporary offices were set up in Womanby Street at a rent of £ 850 p.a for seven years.

Following the war, the tramway replacement programme restarted. Deliveries of new buses were delayed and second hand trolleybuses were bought from Pontypridd to convert the Monument to Pier Head route. The first unique to Cardiff two door pay as you enter double deck trolleybuses started to arrive in 1948 some of the later ones built in Cardiff by Bruce Coachworks at Pengam Moors. The Transport committee examined the first of these to be completed, number 264, on 21 October 1949 at the bodybuilders works. By 1950, enough had been constructed for the last tram to run on 20 February of that year.

Publicity for the pay as you enter system in 1942.

e 'pay as you enter' flat fare system on one of the new trolleybuses in 1942. The fare was one penny for any distance and replaced the zonal fare stem used previously. From 3 May 1942, tram routes were rearranged to terminate in the City centre except workman's specials to allow oduction of 'pay as you enter' on them as well and this was completed by 1 August 1943. It was also introduced on motorbuses on the Splott and morfa routes. The new Cardiff designed trolleybuses from 1948 carried on this system and had two staircases, a front sliding exit door and a seat the conductor on the open rear platform to watch that fares were paid. The flat fare was increased to one and a half pence on 5 June 1949 and ndoned on 12 November 1950, the month the last of these specially designed buses entered service.

"Dad's Army", the Cardiff Corporation Transport Battalion of the Home Guard. During the war, the department was responsible for ARP and Defence vehicles.

n WW II, buses were produced to austerity standards known as Utility by a small number of manufacturers. 75, a five cylinder Guy Arab with Park Royal bodywork entered service in 1944 at a cost of £2280 and lasted until 1960. It's in the overall grey livery that became standard throughout the country. Drivers didn't like them and at first refused to drive them. Although Cardiff had not bought Guys before, they must have made a favourable mpact as a fleet of 96 was bought between 1953 and 1966.

Allied co operation, a US Army grader clears snowbound tram tracks in 1945. Heavy snowfall occurred on 25 January 1945, this may be it.

Doodlebugs to Tiger Bay. A shortage of new Trolleybuses after the war caused the purchase of seven second hand 1930 English Electric trolleybuses from Pontypridd to convert the Monument to Pier Head tram route. Single decks were required to pass under the low Bute Street bridge, another bridge problem. They were replaced in 1949 by single deck versions of Cardiff's standard trolleybus. 231 stands at the Monument, their slow speed, 18 mph, and whining noise earned them their 'doodlebug' nickname, which passed rather unfairly to their successors.

Local wartime supplier Air Dispatch, turned to bus building after the war. Renamed Bruce, in September 1948, their works were in Pengam and they became sub-contractors to East Lancashire coachbuilders of Blackburn. They supplied many buses to Cardiff including trolleybuses, but after the postwar boom, the works closed in 1952. The contact remained and East Lancs provided most of Cardiff's bus bodies up to 1965. 95 is a 1947 AEC Regent II seen outside the City Hall when new. It had less cream on the upper deck and later gained an all over translucent roof. Whilst not repeated, buses from 1961 featured a translucent panel along the centre of the roof.

Roath depot in Newport Road in 1948 with soon to be replaced tram 66 and brand new trolleybus 220. The trolleybus was built by East Lancs works in Blackburn, the Bruce Cardiff built trolleys were constructed about a mile away on Pengam Moors. All were on BUT chassis which was a joint AEC and Leyland company to produce trolleybuses. The electricity generating station is in the background, both monuments to Cardiff's transport history now gone.

Cardiff's last tram, number 11, seen at Gabalfa on 20 February 1950. The General Manager had been granted up to £30 to mark the occasion and the tram was manned by the oldest crew members. They appeared on BBC Welsh Region Radio on 16 January 1950. Three pence souvenir tickets were issued on the tram which ran alongside replacing trolleybuses. It is interesting that both trams and trolleybuses were to a distinctive Cardiff design. As trams used one overhead wire and trolleybuses two, separate wiring had to be provided during joint operation.

I remember when...

The phrase 'a quick cuppa' certainly rang true for Marie Nuth when she was the unofficial tea lady for Cardiff trams along the Crwys Road route in Cathays.

As a teenager in the late 1940s, she worked in her parents' teashop on Crwys Road Bridge.

But her main duty was to brew up for the tram drivers and conductors as their trams passed the shop.

"I would hear a tram giddily swinging up the hill, madly clanging its bell and that was my signal to run out of the shop and meet the conductor," said Marie.

"He would quickly hand me a one pint teacan which had a sixpence piece in it."

Marie had to make the tea and rush back out onto the street to meet the tram as it made its return journey a few minutes later.

"I'd hear the bell ringing again and as the tram approached, I'd hurriedly fill up the teacan and pass it to the conductor.

"The whole process had to be done in seconds and tea would always slosh everywhere. But I really enjoyed making tea for the trams and I'm proud to be a part of Cardiff Bus' history."

Chapter Five: *The Fifties – A new era*

Evocative of the times, morning rush hour at Victoria Park in 1950. Trolleybuses started running here on 6 June 1948, their third route, and 216 is here behind AEC Regent 102 which has an East Lancs lowbridge body. This design featured a sunken gangway on the offside of the top deck with long seats for four people along the nearside. They were very uncomfortable and very difficult for conductors to collect fares. They were necessary to clear low bridges and Cardiff needed them particularly for the long route to Tredegar. The bus in the background is still in wartime grey.

By the time of the Accession in 1952, the Corporation's vehicles were carrying 91,558,978 passengers, running 7,825,105 miles and earning £936,903 in a year

THE temporary offices in Womanby Street were replaced by offices in a former school in Wood Street on 1 June 1950. The Corporation entered an era of returning to normal with the reinstatement of pre-war mileage although there was a period of fuel shortage during the Suez Crisis. Being part of the Municipal Passenger Transport Association, a reduction in the cost of fuel was allowed which in 1950, meant a saving of £375 a year on the 650,000 gallons used. By the time of the Accession in 1952, the Corporation's

vehicles were carrying 91,558,978 passengers, running 7,825, 105 miles and earning £936,903 in a year. In 1954, the City Transport suggested staggering school hours to reduce the burden on peak hour buses. The Education Committee surveyed head teachers, two were in favour and 32 against so no action was taken. The Transport Committee was extremely disappointed. Six new buses in 1959 were the first to be fitted with heaters. As the City grew, so routes expanded outwards serving areas such as Llanrumney and Pentrebane.

Cardiff's buses strayed far afield and 1950 AEC Regent III number 14 is in Castle Street, Merthyr Tydfil. This route was started on 8 September 1930 and was run jointly with Merthyr Corporation and, after initial disagreements about timings, Rhondda Transport. Merthyr complained that Cardiff's buses were not of a suitable standard and a referbished bus was bought from Dennis with a Park Royal body for £446 and 8 shillings. It was examined by the Tramways Committee on 22 December 1930. Number 14 and its 19 sisters were regarded as the flagships of the fleet and cost £ 81, 576 8 shillings and 4 pence in total. This bus, along with four others and five trolleybuses, were sub-contracted to East Lancs' works in Bridlington, a rare occurance for buses sold in the south. They lasted between 16 and 18 years.

In the 1950's, underfloor engined single deckers became the norm increasing seating capacity over the old front engined types by over 30% Cardiff had nine of these, five being 1952 Leyland Royal Tigers with East Lancs 44 seat bodies. One of these,No 134, is seen on Penarth Road on the route to Penarth joint with Western Welsh. They were needed in particular for the very narrow road and low arch bridge near Cogan. For many years, buses had to pay tolls to use Penarth Road, a reduction for bulk use of 25% was agreed in 1935.

Sloper Road inspection pits, 16 February 1953. This was home to the motorbus fleet, trams never visiting it and trolleybuses only being stored or towed there for steamcleaning. Motorbuses were introduced to Roath depot in 1964 and the whole fleet moved to Sloper Road in 1986 following expansion of the site. The bus nearest the camera, No 128, (DUH 315) is a Bristol KW6G, one of 20 and a type only supplied to Cardiff.

Wood Street in 1953 with trolleybuses in evidence around the site that on 6 December 1954 was opened as the bus station, bringing the termini of many routes together. It was rebuilt to its current layout in 1983.
INSET Route map from 1952

In 1955, Cardiff had been a City for 50 years. Trolleybus 208, one of the original Northern Counties bodied AECs of 1942 was decorated accordingly. Cardiff also became the Capital of Wales in that year. Illuminated trolleybuses became part of the Christmas scene in Cardiff and travelling in one through the City Centre Christmas lights was a delight. When these 7' 6" wide buses were withdrawn in the mid 1960's, with No 208 being the very first trolley to go, the replacing illuminated eight footers could only have illuminations on the front.

The annual retired staff outing in 1958 outside the Wood Street offices. Cardiff did not own any luxury coaches until 1976, so transport is provided by the Red & White company.

Cardiff's trolleybuses were fitted with batteries and could run quite a way off the wires. Road improvements which were the end of trolleybuses throughout the UK meant rewiring and the widening of Newport Road is causing East Lancs bodied 216 to turn from City Road under battery power. By now, the bus's front doorway has been panelled over but the two staircases remain. It was a tradition that as the conductor appeared up the back stairs, you would run down the front one to avoid paying the fare.

On 8 May 1955, the last trolleybus extension was made taking them beyond the tram routes to Ely. They ran along Grand Avenue where the large central reservation was for the intended tram service. Thirteen double decks were bought for this and only ever had one door. One additional single decker was bought for the Bute Street route and Cardiff's last two new trolleys are posed here at Green Farm Road terminus in Ely. 287 (KBO 960) and its sisters worked well on into the final days of trolleys, but No 243 (KBO 961) only did nine years work and was only ever used on the Bute Street route. Strangely, Cardiff's last new single deck trams only ran for nine years as well. The total bill for the 14 buses was £ 83,500 and they were part of a contract for 20. The remaining six were ordered as motorbuses in 1961 to start the conversion.

I remember when...

It may have been a dark time for the country, but the World War II blackouts were a memorable time for one Cardiff Bus driver.

Robert Rogers worked on the buses for 40 years, between 1935 and 1975, and witnessed some of the key moments in Cardiff history from the driving seat.

"I'll always remember driving buses through Cardiff during the blackout as it was such a monumental time," said Robert.

"The blackout did cause problems for the buses as it was difficult to drive in complete darkness, but at the same time it reminded me that life had to go on - people still had to get about and the buses had a major part to play in society."

Whenever an air raid siren went off, the bus drivers were told to take their passengers to the nearest shelter.

"It was scary as you never knew what might happen," Robert said.

"And I felt a huge responsibility to make sure my passengers were safe."

Chapter Six: *The buses in the swinging sixties*

Two way radios were introduced for inspectors in 1968

THE decision to replace trolleybuses with motorbuses over a ten year period was taken in 1961. Trolleys were regarded as inflexible and slow at junctions. Longer motorbuses with more seats were used to replace them. Traffic congestion in the City began to have a serious effect on reliability, but the Public Works and Town Planning committee claimed in July 1961 that this was due in part to buses. Bridge problems continued, the Wood Street bridge over the Taff was declared weak on 16 December 1965 and the trolleybuses weighing 15.5 tons were banned from midnight. The 6 and 9 routes to Pier Head stopped at the bus station, lighter motor buses taking over the southern part until the whole routes were converted on 16 April 1966. Then on 1 April 1969, Ely bridge on Cowbridge Road was declared weak almost bringing to an end the last trolleybus route. However bailey bridges were put in and trolleybuses used them, probably the only occasion anywhere that this happened. Two way radios were introduced for inspectors in 1968. Projected losses for 1968/9 were £80,000. Union resistance would not allow driver only operation, so fares had to rise to generate £100,000 of extra revenue. Uncollected fare boxes had been fitted to all buses in June 1951 and by April 1969 had collected a total of £ 9,234, 14 shillings and 7 pence.

The first trolleybus conversion was of services to Pengam in November 1962, ironically caused by a road scheme to a car parts plant. These routes finished very near the Bruce Coachworks factory and were the only ones to pass Roath depot. Thereafter it was out on a limb. Of the 50 Cardiff design 'pay as you enter' double deck trolleys, Bruce built 25 in Cardiff, and East Lancs built 20 in Blackburn and five in Bridlington. The PAYE system was scrapped in November 1950, the same month as Bruce bodied 273 first went on the road, numerically the last but one but the last into service. It may never have been used as intended. It's here at picturesque Llandaff Fields terminus in a later version of crimson lake and cream, training new drivers. Driving trolleybuses was very different and from 1966, when this picture was taken, motorbuses had semi-automatic gears to make the transition easier.

AEC buses had been part of the Cardiff fleet for many years. Brand new No 413 of 1963, with East Lancs body was one of the last AEC double decks bought and is passing a similar Leyland bus one year older in Dorchester Avenue, Penylan. They are on the 24 route which described a huge circle in west Cardiff via Llandaff North and Whitchurch. When it was introduced in 1929, the Corporation had to agree with the Glamorganshire Canal Company that it would run buses at its own risk over the narrow hump back bridge outside the Cow & Snuffers pub in Llandaff North.

A major event for Cardiff in 1965 was the conversion of Queen Street to one way. This required the building of a new link road from Park Place to Dumfries Place and this was wired for trolleybuses. 275 is conveying an official party on a test run followed by one of the department's Bedford overhead repair wagons. Until the early 1960's adverts had to be painted onto the bus and be in the fleet colours of crimson lake and cream. Cardiff's famous brewers, Brains, were a regular supporter and 275 displays a classic example.

From the late 1950's, double deck buses began to move to rear engines. This allowed greater seating capacity, flatter floors, the door could be under the constant supervision of the driver and driver only operation was possible. Cardiff's first 32 vehicles were Daimler Fleetlines that arrived in 1967 at a total cost of £256,767. Here, No 477, is being inspected by the General Manager, Mr E.G.A. Singleton on the right and senior politicans outside the City Hall. It was one of 16 with Metro Cammell bodies of a style supplied to Manchester. The other 16 had Park Royal bodies in Sheffield style.

In the late 1960's, standee type single deckers with two doors became fashionable, more as a result of the likelihood of Union agreement to driver only operation than suitability for the job. After trying an Aberdare bus, Cardiff bought 20 of these AEC Swift rear engined buses in 1968, its last AECs. Apart from three shorter ones in the Lancashire United fleet, this style of Alexander body was another type only found in Cardiff. Route 44 was a limited stop service introduced in June 1969 to give people a faster journey to the City and 507 is seen at Llanrumney roundabout. It was later extended to Ball Road and in March 1970, it and others became driver only operated using these buses.

Cardiff's trolleybuses, like the trams, lasted longer because of late delivery of new buses. They finally stopped running on 3 December 1969 but reappeared for a planned farewell on the weekend of 10/11 January 1970, the only time six wheel trolleys ran in service in the 1970's. The very last one, 262, Bruce built and still in existence as the only remaining Welsh built trolley in the UK is here on the 11 January at Green Farm Road. This was a one way single line extension that one in three 10B trolleys used and was the most westerly trolleybus route in the UK at the time.

I remember when...

Cardiff Bus has really been a family affair for Joan Roberts and her family.

Her grandfather drove one of the horse drawn carriages and of his six sons, four were employed by Cardiff Transport.

His eldest son, William Bishop, was a bus inspector, while his three younger sons, including Joan's father, were bus drivers for all their working lives.

"Our family has worked with buses for generations and I joined the 'family business' when I got a job in the Transport offices in Womanby Street. My father was really proud as it was quite an achievement to work in the offices in the early forties."

And it was through working with buses that Joan met her husband.

"I was the first female clerk to get promotion to the Season Ticket Department and when I arrived at work one morning, I found our offices being picketed by striking bus men."

It was during this strike that Joan became friendly with one of the pickets, John Roberts.

After two years of courting, much of which took place on the buses, they were married.

"John and I have been married for 52 years now," added Joan.

"I really do have a lot to thank Cardiff Bus for."

Chapter Seven: Pick up a Seventies orange

1971 it was decided that a more modern image was needed and the crimson lake and cream livery was replaced by light orange chosen in preference to dark orange or turquoise

WITH the arrival of David Smith as General Manager in 1971, it was decided that a more modern image was needed and the crimson lake and cream livery was replaced by light orange chosen in preference to dark orange or turquoise. The name City of Cardiff was used in English on one side and Welsh on the other. Driver only operation started on St David's Day 1970 using single decks on routes 33, 40A & B, 44 and 54 and was extended to double decks on routes 1, 6, 9, 22 and 23 on 6 June 1971. Full driver only operation was achieved by 1980, the last conductors working the Snowden Road route that April. Decimal money was introduced on D-Day, 15 February 1971. New offices were opened in Wood Street on Wednesday 14 March 1973. Under the local government reorganisation of 1974, control of the buses passed to the new Cardiff City Council. A zonal fare system was introduced in 1974 along with multiride tickets to speed up boarding times. The growing leisure market was addressed in 1976 when the first luxury coach was bought. UK tours, visits to mainland Europe and private hires were undertaken, but it was not sustainable after 1995. During the 1970's, radio control, CCTV and bus lanes were introduced to help ensure reliability.

Cardiff buses

1 City Circle (clockwise)
2 City Circle (anticlockwise)
3 St. Mary St. Heath Hospital Rhydypenau
4 St. Mary St. Lake Rd. East Rhydypenau

10 June 1973 until further notice

1970's timetable

e sixties continued to swing into the early seventies, and Cardiff had the first bilingual psychadelic bus. No 550, the last of 25 1969 Willowbrook
died Fleetlines that saw off the trolleybuses was painted to the order of Silexene paints. Inevitably, the first one was in London, but this was
cond and had the words in Welsh on one side. These buses were the only two door double deck motorbuses and were used to introduce driver
y double decks in 1971. It's outside the City Hall.

The final form of the crimson lake and cream livery is here on Guy Arab 353 of 1958 climbing Ball Road in Llanrumney in the early 1970's. The development of Pentwyn and the M4 are yet to come and the picture demonstrates the growth in the City that its Transport Department has had to deal with over the years.

The three buses in the trial new liveries are lined up outside the City Hall in 1971 as part of the public consultation. Female members of staff, dressed to match each bus, handed out leaflets. The single decker, on the left won.

Bus companies throughout the land painted buses in this silver and blue livery for the Queen's silver jubilee in 1977. Cardiff's was 566, a 1972 Fleetline of the last batch of 92 of the type owned. This had Metro Cammell bodywork and was known to crews with its 34 sisters as a K-liner. They were popular because they were very fast. They were the last new buses delivered in crimson and cream. Also in the picture is a Bristol midibus introduced in 1974 used on a network of routes with narrow residential roads. It is passing an open top Guy Arab bus used on City tours. Although originally introduced in the 1950's, these tours were revamped using open toppers in 1976.

Cardiff's last front engined rear entrance bus ran in 1979. They were part of a batch of 37 Guy Arab Vs delivered in 1966 that marked a departure after many years in having Alexander of Falkirk bodies, again a type believed to be unique to Cardiff. They were also the first buses with two pedal control semi automatic gearboxes. This one, 448, shown new in Falkirk, is one of the 15 longer 70-seaters used to replace trolleybuses, the remaining 22 seating 65. Extra space for prams was provided behind the nearside rear wheel of these at an extra cost of £10 10 shillings per bus. It was subsequently fitted to earlier buses.

DIANA DORS

I remember when...

She may have been more used to limousines and transatlantic jets, but Diana Dors travelled by tram when she came to Cardiff in 1947.

The glamorous film star was the niece of Cardiff Bus driver, Bert Evans, and caused quite a stir when she got on 'Uncle Bert's' tram.

"Diana was quite a young starlett then and had just returned from a trip to America,"

said Ernest Adams, who was the conductor on Bert's tram.

"She was staying with Bert and his wife in Canton and she and her mother had to catch the No 5 tram, Victoria Park - St Mary Street, to get to the station."

At the time, clothes were strictly rationed and purchased with coupons from a ration book.

So the immaculately dressed Diana was bound to attract a few stares.

"I remember Diana and her mother got on the tram, dressed in the best clothes purchased from the top New York shops," said Ernest.

"Diana looked out of this world. She attracted quite a few envious glances and there were some not very pleasant comments from the female passengers.

"But despite that, I found Diana pleasant to talk to and I'm proud that our tram carried a film star."

49

Chapter Eight: *The Twentieth Century draws to a close*

In the late 80's, there was a major increase in the number of midibuses known as 'Clippers' which in turn generated a significant increase in the number of jobs

THE 1980 Transport Act allowed competition for local bus routes and Cardiff buses had its first for over 50 years. The CK company started buses to Cyncoed, Llanrumney and Pentwyn but ceased in 1982. Between 1981 and 1983, fareboxes were introduced on all buses with an exact fare system, a return to the old days ! They were designed to speed up boarding and also reduce the number of attacks on drivers. The old tram depot in Newport Road ceased to run buses in 1980 but stayed in use as a central repair works until 1986 when it was closed. Improved facilities replaced it at Sloper Road and in September 1986 a new head Office was opened there as well. The 1985 Transport Act introduced deregulation from October 1986 and also obliged local authorities to establish "arms length" companies to run their buses. Accordingly the City Council established its own company, Cardiff City Transport Services, which now trades as Cardiff Bus. The Council owns all the shares and is represented on the Board. Cardiff Bus cannot receive subsides and is expected to make a contribution to its shareholder the City Council. In the late 1980's, there was a major increase in the number of midibuses known as "Clippers" which in turn generated a significant increase in the number of jobs. On 19 June 1936, a policy was agreed to replace all single decks with double decks on the grounds of very large cost economies. In the 1990's, this was reversed on the basis that single decks are more environmentally friendly, less obtrusive and suffer less from vandalism. A large expansion into Barry, Caerphilly and the Vale took place in February 1992 when

Optare Excel 'Easyrider' 206, one of the first batch of Cardiff's low-floor, easy-access single deckers for use on the Heath Hospital – Cardiff Bay services where the innovation was much appreciated by passengers. Delivered in 1997, the fifteen buses were sold for further service in Reading as a rationalisation of vehicle types. These buses are now in service with Eastbourne Buses.

the National Welsh company ceased trading. This brought daily passenger journeys to almost 100,000. Further expansion in the Vale came with the purchase in February 1995 of Golden Coaches of Llandow. More competition was experienced on Ely and Rumney routes from 1993 to 1996 from the Cardiff Bluebird company. The last coach tours ran in 1995 and the last open toppers in 1998. The Council became Cardiff County Council in 1996 and the fleetname was adjusted to Cardiff Bus. In 1999, the livery changed once again to the present one of Burges blue and cream. This is Cardiff Council's corporate scheme and the adoption emphasises the link between the two organisations just as the crimson lake and cream did for nearly 70 years.

typical 80's scene of Cardiff oranges leaving the bus station. The bus on the left is a Volvo Ailsa, a front engined model and destined to be the last e of double deck owned by Cardiff Bus. It has bodywork by Northern Counties who were responsible for many 1930's Cardiff buses and the first lleybuses. The other bus is a Bristol VRT, one of a fleet of 117 built up between 1974 and 1980. This is one of 26 with Willowbrook bodywork, who lt the buses that replaced the last trolleybuses.

Second hand buses were used in the 1980's to help replace worn out vehicles. This is a Leyland Atlantean, a type not bought new by Cardiff but very popular with the old Western Welsh company, a forerunner of National Welsh. It came from Plymouth.

Expansion in 1992 brought Cardiff Bus to Barry and greater use of midibuses. A busy scene at the Civic Centre in King Square shows how brown and white had been introduced to the livery. The buses on the left are MCW Metroriders a type favoured by Cardiff. The bus on the right s a Renault bought second hand to cope with the extra routes. It, too, came from Plymouth.

Open top tours were run until 1998. One of the original Daimler Fleetlines number 485, was converted for this work and its here beside the se
at Penarth. It is painted in the old tram livery to celebrate the company's 75th anniversary. Later new convertible open top buses were bough
for this work.

he adoption of the Council's corporate scheme in 1999 harked back to a similar policy with the old crimson lake and cream. Here it is on one of the ngle deck trolleys, number 238, needed for a low bridge on the Bute Street route. It's at the Monument terminus.

I remember when...

As a conductor, and later a driver, of Cardiff's trams and trolleybuses between 1946 and 1958, Ernest Adams says that one of the best parts of his job was getting to meet and know his regular passengers.

As he drove around the city, he saw people going about their day-to-day business, but also shared in some of their special moments.

"I always remember one man who used to catch the tram to court his girlfriend," said Ernest.

"We used to tap twice on the bell as we approached Tydfil Place in Roath to let him know we were coming. We'd then see him coming across the road, out of breath.

"He eventually married his girlfriend and gave some wedding cake to the tram drivers and conductors who had helped him."

Ernest revealed how Cardiff Bus' drivers and conductors were always helping their regular passengers.

"The man who held the keys and opened up Marments store in Queen Street always caught the trolleybus.

"He lived near the Llandaff Fields terminus and needed to catch the 8.04am trolleybus. We would always look out for him and if he wasn't in sight by 8am, myself or one of the other drivers would run round the corner to knock on his door.

"He would then come running up the road and jump on the bus just as we were leaving."

Chapter Nine: *Into the Twenty-first Century*

The investment in terms of money and effort by staff is huge, and will hopefully secure the future of bus travel in Cardiff for another one hundred years

THE modernisation of Cardiff Bus continues apace, with the introduction of new vehicles, technology and working practices. Government targets for emissions, timekeeping, lost kilometres and age of the fleet are stringent, and the company has made progress against all these targets.

All vehicles now run on ultra low sulphur city diesel and, with the introduction of some 85 new single deck vehicles in the past three years, the age of the fleet has been reduced to an average of six years. The new buses are mostly Super Pointer and Midi Pointer Dart, with flat floors and easy access doors. This, combined with the introduction across the routes on which they operate of raised kerb bus stops by the County Council, means that Cardiff Bus offers a service which is more customer focused and suitable for a wide range of user groups.

The introduction in 2001 of new digital radios and satellite tracking means that controllers will be able to pinpoint vehicle movement and traffic flow, and keep passengers up to date with the expected arrival time of the next service via the 'real time information' panels being fitted to bus stops across the City. Buses are also being cleaned more regularly to keep them in better condition. Drivers take their vehicles through the bus washes at the company's Sloper Road Depot each evening, where the cleaners then take care of the interiors. In addition, a 'mid-day sweep out' has been introduced at the Central Bus Station, to freshen up buses during the day as well.

All these improvements to the fleet and operating procedures provide the background for one of the most significant changes to the way Cardiff Bus operates

The service changes introduced for the east of the city in May 2001 required additional vehicles. Fifteen Super Pointer Darts joined the fleet at a cost of around £1.5 million.

since deregulation in 1986. Service improvements were introduced in St Mellons, Pentwyn and Llanrumney in May 2001. More improvements will be introduced in the rest of Cardiff at Easter 2002, and will see more low-floor services and improved frequency across the city, creating a 'shuttle' style service every 10 minutes or more frequently along the city's major routes. The investment in terms of money and effort by staff is huge, and will secure the future of bus travel in Cardiff for another hundred years.

The new easy access vehicles drop down to kerb level to make it easy to get on and off the vehicle either with a pram, on foot or in a wheelchair. The introduction across Cardiff of raised kerb bus stops by the County Council has made it much easier for people to board the buses.

The use of CCTV and radios to monitor traffic flow and vehicle whereabouts is nothing new for Cardiff Bus, but the introduction of satellite technology now means that passengers at bus stops can find out when the next service is due by looking at the information displays being fitted into bus shelters.

The introduction in 2001 of a new state of the art control centre at the company's Wood Street offices makes it easier for controllers to monitor the buses and for drivers to stay in touch via the new digital radios installed on all vehicles. This provides better communications and improved safety for passengers and drivers alike.

Following the introduction of new contractual arrangements for drivers in 2001, they now take the buses through the bus wash themselves at the end of a shift. This has released cleaning staff from that duty, meaning that more staff are available to clean buses every night.

The introduction of the mid day sweep out at the Central Bus Station has been well received by passengers. Having a nice clean bus to use more than makes up for having to wait a short time while the bus is swept through.

The future of Cardiff Bus.
Lee Richardson, a driver with
Cardiff Bus for just over two
years, tied for first place in the
prestigious national UK Driver of the
Year competition 2001, only being
knocked back to second place after a
tie break. Lee put his success down to
the skills and training he had been
given at Cardiff Bus, which offers all
employees the opportunity to
continue with formal training and
education right through their
careers with the company.

ACKNOWLEDGEMENTS

This book does not aim to be a definitive history, it tries to give a flavour of Cardiff's transport over 100 years. Much information has come from Cardiff Corporation minutes and material in the care of the Glamorgan Records Office and the National Museums & Galleries of Wales. Valuable input has come from Gerald Truran, Chris Taylor, Glyn Bowen, Colin Morris, John Woodward and Cardiff Bus. Glyn Bowen, Colin Morris and Mike Strange have provided photos, but the majority are from the Cardiff Bus collection. We know some have been supplied by others for this collection and our thanks go to them. Valuable cross checking was possible with the excellent books 'Cardiff Electric Tramways' by David Gould and 'The Cardiff Trolleybus' by Glyn Bowen and John Callow. Both are commended to you. The work of preserving Cardiff's transport heritage continues with the Cardiff Transport Preservation Group and the Cardiff and South Wales Trolleybus Project. Both could do with your support.

The memories of readers of the South Wales Echo make this a very personal record and I would like to thank journalist Gemma Williams for collating the stories of Ernest and Dorothy Adams, John Hall, Norman Forrest, Marie Nuth, Joan Roberts and Stan Rogers. To South Wales Echo designer, Nick Clarke I extend my thanks for putting up with the inumerable changes that I have made along the way to the text.

In the end, what is in the main body of this book, is down to me. So, for any inaccuracies, I apologise.

Roger Davies
January 2002

Research and Writing
Roger Davies

Design and Printing

Editing and Project Management
goodrelations

© Cardiff City Transport Services Ltd (January 2002)
Leckwith Depot, Sloper Road, Cardiff. CF11 8TB

 **Cardiff Bus**
BWS CAERDYDD

Cardiff Bus and the South Wales Echo are delighted to be able to support the excellent work of both Ty Hafan and the George Thomas Hospice, through the sale of this book. For every book you buy, Ty Hafan and George Thomas will share a £1 donation. Hopefully, we will be able to sell all of the copies printed and raise £4,000 for each of these very good local causes. On behalf of both Ty Hafan and The George Thomas Hospice, I thank you for your support.

Steve Pantak
Chairman, Cardiff Bus

George Thomas Hospice Care is the major provider of home based specialist palliative care to those facing cancer and other life threatening illnesses in Cardiff and the Vale of Glamorgan.

Our specialist nurses, Social Workers and Occupational Therapists care for up to 1,000 local patients and their families each year. The demand for our support, provided totally free of charge, is continually growing.

Your help through donations, legacies, bequests, payroll giving and fundraising events enables us to help others at a most difficult and sensitive time in their lives.

To become a volunteer or learn more about our special work please contact us at:

10 Ty Gwyn Road, Penylan, Cardiff
Tel: 029 2048 5345
E Mail: info@George-Thomas-hospice.org.uk
www.george-thomas-hospice.org.uk

 **GEORGE THOMAS HOSPICE CARE**

Ty Hafan is the only children's hospice in Wales. It provides respite and end of life care both in the hospice and at home for children who suffer from conditions which mean that they will die before they reach adulthood.

Ty Hafan is dedicated to providing love, care and support for the whole family. We offer a listening ear, a helping hand and more. We offer friendship, a sense of community; a sharing in the care of the very sick child; expert respite, palliative and end of life care and bereavement support for the family for as long as it is wanted.

We believe in helping our sick children to make the most of the precious time they have left.

A children's hospice is a place of love and understanding, of fun, hope and friendship. As one Mum said "it is a place for living."

It costs around £1 million every year to maintain this service, which is unique in Wales and completely free to all our families.

For further information or to make a donation, please call the Ty Hafan Appeal Office on 01446 739993 Email: info@tyhafan.org.